I Am Different

by
Crystel Patterson

illustrated by
Briana Young

ISBN-10: 1-956468-03-X
ISBN-13: 978-1-956468-03-8

The "Inspired to be..." book series is a collection of children's books inspired by the culture, experiences, and dreams of Black people with the goal of inspiring all children.

I Am Different is the second book of the "Inspired to be..." Series.

With this book, it is my hope that children are inspired to be confident in themselves and embrace their differences. Despite the mixed reactions they may receive, I hope they'll find a way to focus on the positive and love themselves ALWAYS in ALL WAYS.

MALACHI   Nia   Ekon

There are some things about me
That stand out for all to see.

Some people say words that sting

Others say the very best things.

2

I am different, this I know
I am different and it shows.

With some kids, I don't fit in
I don't think I ever will.

Fit in: to be accepted as part of a group
Have you ever felt like you didn't fit in? How did it make you feel?

3

I am different, this I know
I am different, and it shows.
With my family, I'm a fit
With my friends, I'm a hit!

My skin is different, this I know
My skin is different, and it shows.
Some kids tease me about my skin
And compare it to awful things.

Awful: very bad
Has anyone ever said awful things about you? How did it make you feel?

Tease: to make fun of someone or something
How do you think you would feel if someone teases you about something you
cannot change about yourself?

My skin is different, this I know
My skin is different, and it shows.

My grandma compliments my skin
She thinks it's the most stunning thing!

Compliment: something you say to someone to show that you like a certain thing about them
What are some examples of compliments others have given you or that you have given to someone else?

Stunning: very beautiful or attractive
Do you think your skin is stunning? Why or why not?

My skin is different, this I know
My skin is different, and it shows.

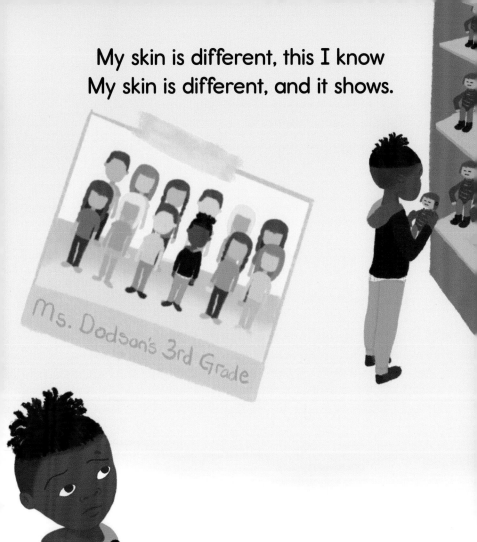

Ms. Dodson's 3rd Grade

So mixed reactions I receive
I wonder who I should believe.

Mixed Reactions: When some people like something while others dislike it.
What are some things you get mixed reactions about?

My hair is different, this I know
My hair is different, and it shows.
Some kids tease me about my hair
When they see it, they tend to stare.

9

My hair is different,
this I know

My hair is different,
and it shows.

My best friend always tells me that
My hair is perfect, that's a fact!

My hair is different, this I know
My hair is different, and it shows.

So mixed reactions I receive
I wonder who I should believe.

My name is different,
this I know
My name is different,
and it shows.

Some kids think my name is strange
They tell me I should change my name.

Strange: different from what is usual, normal, or expected
Do you think it's a bad thing for someone to have a strange name?

My name is different, this I know
My name is different, and it shows.

My sister says my name fits me
She tells me "strong" is what it means!

Strong: not easy to break or damage; able to deal with difficult situations
Why do you think Ekon's sister reminds her that her name means strong?
Do you know if your name has a specific meaning?

My name is different, this I know
My name is different, and it shows.

So mixed reactions I receive
You want to know who I believe?

Not the kids who always tease me
And say all those mean things to me.

Pool Rules

They don't like my name, skin, or hair
But guess what, I simply don't care!

17

I believe those who matter to me

My family and friends who uplift me.

Uplift: to make someone feel good about themselves
Who in your life uplifts you? How do they uplift you?

They always see the best in me
Which is what I see when I look at me!

I say positive affirmations to myself.

That I am

STRONG,

BEAUTIFUL,

CREATIVE,

and

KIND.

Positive Affirmation: statement or phrase you repeat to yourself which describes how you want to be

Why do you think it's important for someone to say positive affirmations to themselves? Do you have any positive affirmations?

I'm loved by the people who matter to me

So, who do I believe? I believe me!

I love my rich, brown skin
I love my full, natural hair
I love my beautifully unique name

I love my friends and family
who love me for me
I love being different,
it's what makes me Me!

Unique: One of a kind
Do you consider your name to be unique? Why or why not?

Now that you have read this book, do you think you are different?
If so, what makes you different?
Why do you think it's okay for someone to be different?

A positive affirmation is a statement or phrase you repeat to yourself which describes how you want to be. Would you like us to create a positive affirmation together?

My Affirmations

I AM

I AM

I AM

I AM

I AM

Glossary

Awful: very bad

Compliment: something you say to someone to show that you like a certain thing about them

Different: not the same

Fit in: to be accepted as part of a group

Mixed Reactions: When some people like something while others dislike it.

Positive Affirmation: statement or phrase you repeat to yourself which describes how you want to be

Stunning: very beautiful or attractive

Strange: different from what is usual, normal or expected

Strong: not easy to break or damage; able to deal with difficult situations

Tease: to make fun of someone or something

Unique: one of a kind

Uplift: to make someone feel good about themselves

This book is inspired by Kheris Rogers who is a role model for any child being teased for being different. In 2017, at just 11 years old, she became the youngest fashion designer to feature her work at New York Fashion Week. She was teased for her dark skin complexion in school, which inspired her to start her own clothing line, Flexin' in My Complexion, and encourages people to love their skin.*

This book is also intended to teach new words and phrases and start important discussions.

****

If you enjoyed this book, please take some time to leave a review on Amazon. Your review makes a huge difference and will help other readers discover this book too.

Thank You!

*Biographical information on Kheris Rogers cited from
https://www.businesswomen.org/2017/09/kheris-rogers-youngest-fashion-
designer-ever-new-york-fashion-week-flexin-in-my-complexion.html

Photo by Kenneth McRae

Crystel is a mother to two beautiful boys, a wife, a Technology Consultant, and a self-published author.

In January 2021, she published her first children's book, which kicked off her "Inspired to be..." children's book series. The "Inspired to be..." book series seeks to spread Black inspiration to ALL children through stories based on the culture, experiences, and dreams of Black people. Each story in the series delivers a universal message that any child can relate to and is inspired by a real person so that children will have a point of reference and can say, "If they can do that, then so can I".

To learn more about the "Inspired to be..." series visit www.crystelpatterson.com

Make sure to check out these other books in the "Inspired to Be..." series: